Gus Greenbear
&
the Beijing Fortune Cookie Caper

Also by Peggy C. Hall

Gus 'n Us
(with Frank Wendeln)

In Case of Bears

Techno Poetry: Seasonal Amnesia & Not Always What It Seems

Also by Sandra Riley

Homeward Bound: A History of the Bahamas to 1850

The Lucayans

Stone Poems/Wotai: Help on the Way

The Greenbear Chronicles

Sisters of the Sea:
Anne Bonny and Mary Read—Pirates of the Caribbean

Sometimes Towards Eden: Anne Bonny in Jamaica

Bahamas Trilogy: Miss Ruby, Matt Lowe, Mariah Brown
A Collection of Historical Solo Dramas

Gus Greenbear
&
the Beijing Fortune Cookie Caper

BY

SANDRA RILEY & PEGGY C. HALL

STORY ILLUSTRATIONS BY

ALEX DREXLER
&
AAREN JOHNSON

PARROT HOUSE

2011

PARROT HOUSE

Gus Greenbear and the Beijing Fortune Cookie Caper
COPYRIGHT © 2011 BY SANDRA RILEY AND PEGGY C. HALL

Visit our website at www.rileyhall.com

Library of Congress Cataloging-in-Publication Data is available.
ISBN#978-0-9846191-0-8

First Published January 2011

Original Cover Painting by Mark Runge
Illustrations by Alex Drexler & Aaren Johnson
Book Layout, Cover Design and Cast Portraits by Frank Wendeln
Scrapbook Photos by Mark Runge

To all the Lady Violets in our lives

TABLE OF CONTENTS

From the Authors

"Gus ready to go to China with Mark." This sentence in Peggy's daily Creative Log for February 17, 2002 was the beginning of a deep interest in the literature, art, history and culture of China that culminated in this publication, the fifth one featuring our teddy, Gus Greenbear. Peggy had just completed a poem about "Grizzled Gus," entitled "Lady Fern and the Three Green Bears," a 216-line mock-romance grounded in medieval culture and literary conventions. It was not of epic length, but delusional proof that Peggy could sustain a lengthy original work.

In 2010, eight years later, we offer our thanks and a list of the benefits we received from our research, our experiences in Miami's Asian community, and our collaboration with a circle of friends and artists.

ix

The Fun Stuff

- hours, days, weeks of voluminous, sometimes surreal Internet research on all topics Chinese

- conversational tidbits about Asia deeper than the animal-zodiac placemats at The New Chinatown Restaurant (Peggy is a horse; Sandra and Gus are tigers) and way beyond pandas or Tibet's troubles

- visits to Lucky Oriental Mart in Miami, for red "good luck" envelopes, gold paper money, poetic couplets on paper cutouts, strange but wonderful holiday goodies

- a Chinese New Year's party (Year of the Rat 2008) we threw for our U.K. friends Steve and Chrissy Cronan who, inexplicably, wanted to "eat with chopsticks, from those cute, little take-home paper boxes we see in smart American movies set in NYC"

- the spectacular Beijing Olympics 2008

- heartfelt respect for the ancient traditions of China, as well as their remarkable achievements in all aspects of modern society

- insights into today's China, in real, e-mail time, from the inquisitive, talented artist/martial-arts student—Mark Runge—and his imaginative side-kick and inveterate explorer—Gus Greenbear

- another impressive painting on wood (this one 4'x4') by Mark Runge, with Gus astride a Chinese warhorse, wielding his weapon-of-choice, the Kwan Do, created after their journey to China

Peggy Really Gets Serious

- an introduction to Robert Van Gulik's Judge Dee mysteries, with their exotic details of life in 7th century China. We've read them all!

- acquisition of the visually stunning, textually invaluable *Three Thousand Years of Chinese Painting* (Barnhart, Yale UP, 1997)

- a loan from Mark Runge's library of essential Chinese classics such as *Journey to the West, Romance of the Three Kingdoms: A Historical Novel,* and *Outlaws of the Marsh*

- an exploration of Chinese myths and folktales that parallel so many European stories such as Robin Hood

More Fun Stuff

- an opportunity to work with Alex and Aaren, Mark's art students

- a chance to meet with friends Cecy, Laverne, Travis, Chris and Pattie to read the story aloud, trying not to bother anyone twice and grateful for their company and comments

- another chance to work with Frank on a book design and layout and nearly drive him crazy

x

In Brief

Using Mark's e-mails and photos from China as a base, Peggy began a draft of their adventures. But she wanted to cast it in a form she hadn't written—poetic drama. Aside from infrequent "poetic" passages and scattered haiku (all satiric), the material stubbornly remained episodic, plotless, basically a . . . what? Comic scenes? Travelogue? History lesson? Satire? Graphic sketches? It wasn't a poem, certainly not a drama. Finally, after several drafts, Peggy took some advice from a Chinese fortune cookie: "You are in your own way—please stand aside." She turned over the pieces and parts to Sandra, who caught on to the cookie magic. After much chopping and rewriting, bothering friends with reading and re-reading, the work emerged as a mystery primarily, while retaining (proudly!) its trans-genre-ed quality. Since teddies are trans-gendered, it seems fitting that their playlet has multiple facets. We hope you agree.

PAW NOTES

As Artistic Director of the Parrot House Hug Players, Gus Greenbear encourages all Thespians to read out loud, or to do a full-out performance of this story, royalty free. However, there are a few conditions:

First, colorblind casting is a must. Being green himself, Gus is very sensitive about this, especially now that he has gone a bit gray. Except for Mark, all the characters in the story are teddies who live at or visit the Parrot House Hug (PHH) in Miami, Florida.

Second, the characters may be played by either male or female persons. Teddies in Gus' Hug and in his adventure stories have no gender issues. Feel free to change the pronouns.

Third, Gus advises that there are also a few things to keep in mind about teddies. Their sense of time, or place is non-linear. They go anywhere, in any time period and except for the few artist bears in the Hug who are one-of-a-kinds, they have cousins all over the world who look exactly like they do.

Fourth, teddies in the Parrot House Hug play themselves until called upon to don a costume to suit particular roles required in Gus' plays. In this story Imperial robes are required. The costume shop scurried around, but could not get all the costumes built fast enough for the illustrators to use. Gus changes his mind a lot and tends to make up the story as he goes along. Parrot House actor-teddies are used to this. They can play multiple roles at the drop of a hat, but the technician-teddies in the scene, costume and prop shops go bonkers.

The Parrot House Hug Players begs your indulgence regarding these issues, and encourages audiences to exercise their imaginations and to understand that for Gus, every moment is an adventure.

TEDDY TIME

Anyone who lives with a Teddy Bear knows that in the world of the stuffed people the concept of time has special meaning. We humans small and large, young and old, carry on internal monologues and even hold dialogues in our heads all day long and so do the stuffed people. They know exactly what we are thinking and respond, sometimes loudly when we aren't paying attention. They don't even have to be in the same room with us and we know what they are thinking. We could be at the drug store and hear Gus say, "Bring home some gummie bears." We hold spoken conversations with Gus, when no other humans are around to hear and cart us away to Chattahoochee. Teddies are time travelers the way H. G. Wells understood the term. Physically present with Mark in China in 2002, Gus meets several prominent figures in China's nearly 5000 year old history. Teddies are eternal, universal, wise and they share, allowing mere mortals like ourselves to write down their adventures. This is the latest Gus adventure.

CAST OF CHARACTERS

(Parrot House Hug position and character(s) each plays in the story)

GUS GREENBEAR
Hug Boss, novelist and poet. GENERAL KWAN YU, god of war. (Gus tends to cast himself as the hero in his stories.)

MARK
Art teacher; student of the martial arts; veteran of the First Gulf War.

MAI SHU
Defector from China,
humble proud member
of the Shanghai Panda
Youth (SPY) and Shanghai
Bearpaws Bearball Team.
YELLOW EMPERBEAR,
first Emperbear of China.

ROSIE BEARA
Captain of the PHH Bearball
Team. MAID, a commubear
and DRAGON LADYBEAR,
Dowager Empress of China.

TEN-TEN
A native of Great Britain and frequent honored guest of the PHH until bearports became bearinoid about Denhug Security. COMRADE ARTIST, teacher of traditional Chinese art.

STUART LITTLE
PHH Bearball Team Manager. #1 RAT, Palace Chamberbear.

WINNIE THE POOH

Fish, honey and huckleberry forager for the PHH. PU-I-WIN, small, but last Emperbear of China.

TACO DOG

PHH guard dog. FU-I-DOG, Palace Guard and retainer to Dragon Ladybear.

WEE BEARS

Teddies in disguise in the PHH. WEI BROTHERS, retainers to Dragon Ladybear and tutors for Pu-I-Win. They also play the cubs at the Shaolin Temple Cub School.

Wee Dino plays WEI DINO, archaeologist.

Chilly plays WEI-SEE-SNOW, snow angel instructor.

Scuba Steve is construction boss for the PHH's Habeartat Outreach Program. He plays WEI-FIS-YU, dive master who lost his wet suit, snorkel and fins rescuing Wee Sweet Pea during a tsunami. (At least that's the story he's sticking to in China.)

LADY VIOLET
Gus' special ladybear. MADAMA BEARTTERFLY.

SHIRLEY HOLMES
PHH Security Czar. JUDGE DEE,
Chief Magistrate to Dragon Ladybear
and COMRADE TEACHER at the
Shaolin Temple Cub School.

GREELEY
Hug security guard.
GREENSON BEAR,
retainer to
General Kwan Yu.

NELSON
Hug security guard.
GREENSQUIRE BEAR,
retainer to
General Kwan Yu.

ROSIE-THE-RIVETER
Hug maintenance and
Motherbear's right arm.
GENERAL KWAN YIN.

B. J. THE PIRATE
A visitor from Brandy's tent
at the Pirates in Paradise
Festival in Key West.
B. J. THE PIRATE KING.

GUS GREENBEAR AND THE BEIJING
FORTUNE COOKIE CAPER
ILLUSTRATIONS BY: ALEX DREXLER
AND AAREN JOHNSON

Places in and around Beijing, China provide the backdrop for the story. For Mark the time is 2002, but Gus Greenbear and his friends dip into China's ancient past as though it were an ageless honey pot, perfect food for their imaginations.

On a Plane Leaving China

CAPTAIN DALE: *(Voice over loudspeaker.)* This is Captain Chris Dale. Welcome to Northwest Flight #888 from Beijing, China to Tampa, Florida. Please fasten your seatbelts and enjoy the ride.

GUS

(Writing in his scratchbook.)

We were not as young as New Year's rain, nor as old as autumn's dry leaves when Mark and I journeyed to Bearjing, China. Teddies don't usually return to the place where they began. But, like any bearbrain sensibly stuffed, no matter how far they are shipped, say to Bearattle, Denbear, even Bearami, teddies always carry traces of the Far East. Maybe a bearly remembered peek into an ancient past . . .

MARK
(Stretching and closing his eyes.)
. . . A glimpse of Peking-duck passion . . .

GUS
. . . maybe a single verse about
bamboo shoots or plum blossoms . . .

MARK
. . . Or cranes . . .

GUS
. . . Cranes were already high in the skyscraper
Bearjing sky, building toward the Summer
Olympics, Year of the Rat, 2008. What was
I saying? We were not as young as the first,
fresh, spring rain, nor as old as the last
summer sun when we were in beautiful Bearjing
in the Year of the Horse, 2002. Yet even on
this plane going back to the United States of
Abearica, some tiny grains of Gobi Desert
cling to my green fur . . .

(Yawns.)

MAI SHU
(To himself.)
On calm city streets
                    the dusty sun drops
              flakes of last light
                          on ancient earth bears.

MARK
(Writing in his sketchbook.)

Day 63 Tuesday April 23rd 2002
Two minutes. I go to the bathroom and return to find this
panda in my seat by the window, one furry black arm
stuffed into the corner, the rest of him hidden under my
jacket. And Gus? Asleep-feeling a bit unraveled on our long
flight home, after two months in a foreign culture. Long
days away from his job as Hug Boss and his sweetbear . . .

9

GUS
. . . Lady Violet.

MARK
The man on the aisle barely looked up as I scrunched past,
even when I gathered the two teddies in my lap and tried
to read the Chinese characters on the panda's tag. Probably
means, "No export from China." A stowabear? Cub without
a cave? Uh oh, a bear without a country. What's with the
traditional silk jacket, jade necklace, and why is this
panda wearing motorcycle goggles?
(Rummaging.)
Wonder if he has a bike stashed somewhere?

(Yawns.)

MAI SHU

Button eyes belie
      reality of pool's deeps
           or soul's night disguise.

(Mark, Gus and Mai Shu drop off to sleep.)

TAMPA INTERNATIONAL AIRPORT

(Mark and Gus are writing an e-mail.)

MARK
```
Day 1 Wednesday February 20th 2002.
Dear loved ones.
We are at the airport in Tampa waiting to board our
plane to Beijing. Gus looks smart in his red sweater.
```

GUS
```
And Mark looks handsome in his Lucky-Ducky T-shirt.
```

MARK
```
We plan to fill our travel journal sketchbooks...
```

GUS
```
Scratchbooks.
```

MARK

... with impressions of the sites we visit in and around Beijing. This trip to China is part of our evolution.

GUS

It's a once-upon-a-time opportunity for us visionbearies.

MARK

We miss you already. Our greatest pleasure will be sharing every one of our adventures with you when we return in April, hairier, but closer to "The Three Perfections" of Chinese art: calligraphy, painting, and ...

GUS

Poetry.

MARK

And poetry. We are also determined to work toward leaner, more disciplined bodies by learning new forms of the martial arts.

GUS

As well as the ancient forms of the fine arts.

MARK

Big smiles and lots of love to all in Tampa.

GUS

Endless blessings to you Revered Motherbear, dearest Lady Violet and the Parrot House Hug in Bearami.

XI JIAO HOTEL, BEIJING, CHINA

MARK

Day 2 Thursday February 21st 2002
Evidently a mix-up, something happened with the dormitory
room where we were set to live. I had read that the dorm
hotels have a squatty kind of commode in the shower. I giggled
at that. But I didn't complain too loudly when we were moved
into the Xi Jiao Hotel, designed for Westerners. Pretty fancy
lobby, and we have a neat little room.

GUS

While Mark was checking out the hotel "facilities," and the
TV, and already fretting about getting a special card to use
their laundry, when and where they might serve the free
breakfast he had heard rumors about, I was in charge of
important things like the view from our window, organizing
my little books and art-work space (Mark tends to spread
out a lot), selecting the right art supplies and trail mix for
my knapsack "studio" for upcoming classes, making sure
that the lucky-Ducky comforter Mark brought along fits our
bed and it did. One of us needs to be organized.

MARK

We investigated the campus of the Beijing Language and Cultural University,
which is sort of next door to the hotel. We'll get most meals there.

GUS

I wanted to hang out by the hotel swimming pool, but Mark was thinking
it was way too cold out there.

MARK

I better make it my mission to buy an apple cap soon. I'm a Florida boy
and it's winter in Beijing. I know Gus misses the warm weather also, but
get him to admit it? Swimming, indeed!

YUANMING YUAN
LANDSCAPE GARDENS

MARK

Day 3 Friday February 22nd 2002

It's scary out here. I wish I knew more Chinese. I carry the hotel's address so we can get home. Gus rides in my front jacket pocket so he can see where we are going and what we are doing and who we are meeting and how the Chinese world looks. We walk and walk, sometimes too far. But we are eager to begin seeing Beijing before university classes start.

This morning two Red Guard police with clubs eyed us up as we left the hotel. For a moment, it was flashback city. My first arrest protesting in D.C. with the Vets Against the War.

GUS

I saw all these Chinese vendors in the open markets on the streets with lots of warm caps. But Mark just kept walking.

MARK

We walked for over four hours to a ruined garden the British and French armies tried to destroy in 1860. We were the only Westerners there. Many, many Chinese gave us odd looks.

GUS

I wasn't surprised. I knew they weren't afraid of pandas, but I figured green bears must be a different story.

MARK

I sketched some remnants of a statue called the Fairy Fountain while Gus worked on a rough watercolor of a bright green bonsai-looking tree near the restored pagoda.

His work is decent, considering he's young. He'll learn fast once we begin class.

MARK: *(Looking at Gus' watercolor.)* Gus, little buddy, you've made a good bearginning in your Chinese scratchbook.

MARK

I moved on down the path to look at a ruined pagoda in a stand of wild bamboo.

GUS: Ai-ee! *(Sounds like "hai.")* My watercolor seems too . . . too primitive, too Grandbear Moses. How do you say "bad bear art" in Chinese?

MAI SHU: Hai! No worry. Your Abearican speech quite close to Intercontinental Bearnese. You make slight adjustment then you can talk to teddies in Chinatowns all over world. Just say "Hai!" when begin to speak. Also carry Little-red Bear-book in paw, to flash at Red Bear Guards at den hug gates. *(Bowing.)* I am Mai Shu, mean Walking Bamboo, humble proud member S.P.Y., Shanghai Panda Youth, assigned by Bearnese government hug to reeducate all bears losing esteemed Bearnese heritage after export to Abearica.

GUS: But I am Abearican not Bearnese. My tag says "Russ Bears of New Jersey USA." Oh, hai! I have no Little-red Bear-book. My passport in my bearpack says Bearami, Florida USA. See?

MAI SHU: Hai! Let me prove point you Bearnese inside deep. Check fine print on any tag or box or stop any bear on trail and ask. I say, Miss, hai! Who are you?

MAID: Hai! I am Maid. See tag? Say "Made in China." I go to New York in Abearica when young. Join famous bearball club. I am known in Brooklyn as Rosie Beara. I come back to China. Take care of ancient ones who cannot be rebeared but live in Retirement Village where they sing old songs like "Teddy Bears' Picnic," while they tai chi or dancey-dancey to "Let Me Be Your Teddy Bear" by Elvis before he get chubby and look like Laughing Buddha.

MAI SHU: We learn much Bearnese wisdom from moldy-goldies in China. Rebeared pandas like to follow Tao.

MAID: And quote Confuse-us who say: "See far, but keep at least two paws on ground."

MARK

On the way back to the hotel, Gus surprised me by jumping out of my pocket when he saw this huge roller maybe once used for road work but now turned into an "art" object that lives in a neighborhood park. Gus must have spent ten minutes pushing against it, muttering under his bear breath.

GUS: *(Muttering.)* Take that you Foo Bear and that you Foo Dog!

MARK

Either he's working out or trying to stay grounded or both? When I noticed him rubbing his belly on the way home, I joked.

MARK: Hey Little Buddy, hungry again? Are you trying out for the role of Laughing Buddha? You gotta lay off the fortune cookies.

GUS: What fortune cookies? Now that's interesting. We've eaten a couple restaurant meals and there are no fortune cookies.

MARK: You're right. We've not been served one fortune cookie.

GUS: You gotta admit that's odd. I mean here in Bearjing of all places restaurants should serve fortune cookies. All kinds of fortune cookies, some filled with raspberry jam, peanut butter, blueberry custard …

MARK: Get a grip, Little Buddy.

MARK

Once Gus settled down we watched the news on Chinese TV, and you-know-who's President sounded just as blockheaded in Chinese. Gus made popcorn, but I declined. I can't wait to start kung-fu training. I know I've gained weight. I'm kinda glad there are no fortune cookies in China.

OUT AND ABOUT

GUS: Mark, now that you've bought a cap to keep the extra special cold off your head, let's go to the Zoo and visit the bears.

MARK: I've just signed on for some electives. We're doubling up on calligraphy and painting.

GUS: What are you thinking?!

MARK: We can keep warm in class. It's March and extra special windy outside and beautiful Beijing is dirty.

GUS: What do you expect when the wind from Sibearia brings his friend the dirt from the Gobi Desert and they play in the streets?

MARK: Poets!

GUS: I'm going to spend some quality nap time on the Lucky-Ducky comforter.

MARK: Well, I'm going to the University's art gallery.

GUS
That night Mark kept waking me up.

MARK: The art here in China is the same in America. Some good. Some bad. At the gallery I asked the guide why the student paintings were so Western. She said the students were studying oil painting, and oil painting is Western. Silly me.

GUS: *(Muttering.)* Yeah, silly you.

MARK: Some of the student art here is of the caliber of Yale's art school. And much like Yale, they are very traditional. But they are not traditional Chinese, rather they are traditional Western artists. Go figure.

GUS: Yeah, go figure.

MARK: Why, the whole country could be America. The obvious differences are the language, food, and price of stuff. Stuff here is just plain cheap. I think modern theorists put too much credence in language. Language does not create a people, it merely identifies them. People create language.

GUS

I missed a lot of what Mark was saying about language and how our honey-money really goes a long way in Bearjing market places, but I was wide awake when he said . . .

MARK: So I found a part-time job teaching English.

GUS

Then he turned over and went to sleep. Turns out he'll be teaching the employees of a box company a couple of nights a week.

MARK: You know Little Buddy, I told the woman that I speak American. She just smiled and nodded.

GUS: Sixty people is too many in one class.

MARK: I told her I imagine some will drop out once I start smacking knuckles with my ruler. I am The Foreign White Devil! The woman nodded and said they will pay 100 yuan an hour. It will be perfect. The extra money will see us through the rest of our trip. Gus, teach me the alphabet song. I'm a little rusty.

GUS: Only if you take me to the Bearjing Zoo.

MARK: You got a deal.

GUS: Yahoo!

MARK: No, Gus. Army soldiers say "hooah." Though my energy bar says "oorah!" Probably a Marine thing, but I like it. It has more punch. Oorah! And kick. Oorah!

GUS: *(Reading.)* The guidebook says to pay attention to the signs at the Zoo, especially the one that says, "Real bears don't hug." Think that's true, Mark?

MARK: 'Fraid so, Gus.

RETURNING FROM THE ZOO

GUS

Usually on our walks home at night, I barely look up. I've only seen one star since I've been here. But tonight we saw gobs of stars!

MARK

So we did some paintings about them.

MARK: Gus, I think old Vincent was on to something when he painted at night by the night's light.

GUS: He should have kept his ear, though.

A PUBLIC PARK

MARK

Day 24 Friday March 15th 2002
Chinese language, calligraphy, painting, poetry, martial arts. So many classes. Oorah! And lots of walking. We like to explore the neighborhoods, mingle with the people and eat in the open markets.

GUS

At every stand I asked for a fortune cookie and got a soggy dumpling. One night, walking back to the hotel from school, we went a different way. Small shops with bright flashing lights showered the darkening streets in red, blue, yellow, green …

MARK: I'm not sure we're headed in the right direction.

GUS

I let Mark worry a bit. I could have told him bears have a special BPS system to guide them. Wasn't it bears who first crossed from Asia to Abearica over the Bearing Straits? Anyway, I knew we were okay because I caught glimpses of Mai Shu in the shadows.

MARK

I was relieved when we came to a familiar park, where we had watched people gather in the mornings to do their tai chi, circles upon circles, and other stuff. Tonight, a throng of guys was gathered around two men sitting under a street light. They were locked in battle. Chinese chess, I guess.

GUS

I really couldn't see too well, so I jumped from Mark's pocket and bearreled into the crowd.

MAI SHU: Hai, Gus! It's Mai Shu. Let's go across the park and watch my hug's team the Shanghai Bearpaws finish their semifinal game with the Bearjing Bruins. The winner goes to the Sibearian bearball finals.

GUS: Okay, follow me. I'll get us through this crowd.

MARK

I followed Gus and that other guy. Gus was using the new bagua skills we had learned in kung-fu class. Circle, circle with hands.

GUS

I moved in yin-yang circles like the dragon I drew in my scratchbook.

MARK

The older guys on the edge of the crowd recognized our kung-fu moves and began to open up, the younger guys followed suit. The group parted to avoid the bald, American man and the small green teddy bear spinning through their territory.

GUS

One of the players became so excited he jumped up! A hushed "Awwwwwww" washed through the crowd as the board that was resting on his knees flew up into the air. Each piece on the board leaped into space in a different direction. The crowd roared and stirred and turned on us.

26

MARK
I moved in to save Gus.

GUS
I moved in to save Mark.

MARK & GUS
And we ran off really fast.

MAI SHU: *(Calling after them.)* From now on, bold green bear, you will be known as Mai Long, mean Walking Dragon. And your bareheaded companion will be known as Mai Zhang Yang, Soldier Who Walks in the Sun. We are brothers, we three named Mai. Family dynasty name first. Chinese rule.

MARK

Day 25 Saturday March 16th 2002

Today, we heard through the neighborhood busybodies that
a chess match that had been going on for a record time had
been interrupted last night by a kung-fu demonstration by an
unknown number of masters. The men were very impressed,
and, as it turns out, secretly glad to have the match end as
it did.

PAINTING CLASS

MARK

Day 31 Friday March 22nd 2002
Since we are feeling pretty good and strong in our martial-arts classes, we have decided to help each other focus on our weaker skills.

GUS: *(Pointing to Mark.)* Painting.

MARK: *(Pointing to Gus.)* Poetry. Wait. That's not right.

GUS: *(Pointing to Mark.)* Poetry.

MARK: *(Pointing to Gus.)* Painting.

MARK & GUS: He needs help!

MARK

In our traditional-Chinese-painting-class today, we worked on a small, rice-paper scroll. First, we practiced brush strokes for depicting bamboo. Then, we used an ink stone for light washes.

GUS

Next, we created a short, original poem, to be written in our finest calligraphy right on the scroll. I wrote:

Bamboo stands like brush

Longing for the paints of spring

Not a bear-black cave.

MARK

Our teacher, Comrade Artist Ten-Ten, asked me to think up a Chinese-seal name for myself, to put the finishing touch to my scroll. For some reason, the only name that entered my mind was something like Yin-Yang Mai … no, Mai Zhang Yang, which seems to mean Sunny Soldier?

GUS

Ten-Ten liked the Chinese-seal name I chose. With no hesitation, no doubts . . .

GUS: Mai Long, Walks the Dragon.

TEN-TEN: Walking Dragon.

GUS: Yeah. What was I thinking? Walks the Dragon. Pretty funny image when you think about it.

GUS

I quickly did my seal name in calligraphy. I was way ahead of Mark.

29

MARK

My bamboo brush strokes were so much better drawn than you know whose. I didn't tell Gus that. I also didn't tell him how amazed I was by the difficulty in writing a hokku, ancestor of the haiku. I thought it would be easy. I'll have to do secret homework on poetry.

GUS

Our teacher, Ten-Ten, told me I would have to stay in the bearginner's painting class longer, since my bamboo pawstrokes are too beastly and my calligraphy is just bearable. But then he smiled and said . . .

TEN-TEN: However, there is promise in Greenbear's poetry. It sings barrenness of bamboo in winter snow outside den. Very good for Western bear first time come back to China. I speak as humble panda self. My name, Ten-Ten, mean only ten in whole world. I was created by modest unnamed bear artist. We have one tiny flaw in Ten Dynasty. Bear artist stuffed ball bearings into, beg your pardon, beartocks, to help sitting balance, which turned out to give whole dynasty problems in later life. *(Seeing Mai Shu enter.)* Mai Shu will tell you.

MAI SHU: Since all bearports are now bearinoid about Denhug Security, Ten-Ten can no longer be the world traveler he once was. Every single tiny ball bearing in beartocks sounds alarm at security gates.

TEN-TEN: Sister Ten-One now stranded in Bearmingham, Ten-Two trapped in Bearlin, *(Growing more and more agitated.)* Ten-Seven suspected in plot to invade South Bearolina. So now all Tens must sit on lead butts looking at ancestor portraits of forebears.

MAI SHU: *(Interrupting.)* Hai, Comrade Artist Ten-Ten, it is time for me to escort Abearican friends to The Forbearden City. Bearocrats have scheduled meeting with Dragon Ladybear. She requests honorable Greenbear's presence to become tutor for small nephew Pu-I-Win, Last Emperbear of China.

30

THE FORBIDDEN CITY

RAT: *(Announcing quickly, loudly.)* Hai! I am Rat #1 sign in Bearnese astrology. My time comes again #1 Year of the Rat in 2008. I was #1 Rat 1996, 1984, 1972, 1960, 1948, 1936, 1924, 1912 . . . *(Loses track.)* ah, ah, #1 Rat many times. Now, make way for new tutor of Pu-I-Win, small, but Last Emperbear of China. Bow three times muzzles to earth for honorable teacher, Western name Gustave Greenbear, "Gus" to Revered Motherbear, but now called Mai Long, Walking Dragon. Kowtow on red bearpath to Walking Dragon, Western master bareback merry-go-round rider, almost master of kung fu, not yet good but almost bearable calligraphy. Born Year of Tiger. *(Growls, unconvincingly like a tiger.)* Walking Dragon comes here to Forbearden City to teach small, but last Emperbear all manner of good works from West. So many Decidings proclaimed by the I.G.W. *(Pronounced "Dub-yah.")*, pardon, ah yes, the I.G.B.W. International Good Bears of the World.

DRAGON LADYBEAR: *(Impatiently.)* Ah so, and so, and so. Hai! Walking Dragon. Forgive Palace Chamberbear, name Stu-art from very clean and organized World of Disney, of large boo-boo in linking you to G. Dubyah. I am Dragon Ladybear, Empress Dowager of Embearial China, and Himalayan Moon Bears, Yellow and Yangtze River Bears, Chicago Bears . . . ten thousand pardons. Loose bearings. I mean lose bearings.

GUS: *(Aside to Mai Shu.)* Stuart is Columbia Pictures, not Disney.

RAT: *(Claps his hands.)* Come, teddies! All teddies! Line up. Mind your B's and Q's! Queue up cubbearers, to pass before and make welcome new tutor Walking Dragon and his attendant Comrade Mai Shu. As Confuse-yu say . . .

PU-I-Win: No, not Confuse-yu, Confuse-us! Confuse-us say . . . you're fired! Leave our presence. I introduce self. *(Bows.)* I am Pu-I-Win, small, but last Emperbear of China. Humble kinsbear to wise teddie you call Winnie Pooh who write famous scroll *The Tao of Pooh*.

MAI SHU: *(Aside to Gus.)* Confuse-us speak airy-beary words from clouds.

PU-I-WIN: No, no, Master Confuse-us not airy-beary. Yes, he is beary old, before Tao, but Confuse-us gentle teacher of bear no violence. Teach to live with soft bear nature in small den harmony. Confuse-us say,

"Give hugs a chance," "There's no den like home sweet den," "Ask not what your den can do for you." Forgive, lose bearings. Like you, Greenbear, I study to learn The Three Bearfections: painting, calligraphy, poetry and Bearnese traditions from three wise ones: Confuse-us, Pooh-Tao, and Blessed Bearddha from Bearindia.

DRAGON LADYBEAR: *(Pointing to the wee bears.)* Small Emperbear also learn much from these three wise Wei Brothers. *(To Mai Shu.)* Please introduce.

MAI SHU: Wei Dino.

WEI DINO: *(Bows.)* Hai! I teach small Emperbear to dig for dragon bones.

MAI SHU: Wei Fis-Yu.

WEI-FIS-YU: *(Bows.)* Hai! I teach small Emperbear to swim and dive like fishing bear.

MAI SHU: Wei-See-Snow.

WEI-SEE-SNOW: *(Bows.)* Hai! I teach small Emperbear to make angel bears in snow time.

MAI SHU: *(Aside to Gus.)* Don't let their size fool you. They may be beary small, but word on Yellow River Road is Wei brothers fight like grizzly bears. We commubears watch close.

GUS: *(Bowing.)* Your Imbearial Highness Dragon Ladybear, this insignificant person is greatly honored to tutor Win-I-Pooh, oops Pu-I-Win, small, but last Emperbear of China. Wise Dragon Lady, I beg an answer to something that has been troubling me. Where are the fortune cookies?

Everybeardy gasps!

DRAGON LADYBEAR: Long, long ago, Song Dynasty maybe, Wonton, Egg Drop, Ming dynasty? Who knows? Recipe stolen from Imbearial kitchen. Never found.

GUS: That's it, that's all? No problem. When I return to Bearami, I will go to the New Chinatown Restaurant, write down the recipe in my scratchbook and e-mail it to you. Takes a minute.

DRAGON LADYBEAR: No, no, no. If you have fortune cookie in Abearica it's a knock off. Not same as recipe written on 5000 year old scroll. What you mean e-mail?

FU-I-DOG: *(Bursting in.)* Hai! Humph-aarf! Humph-aarf! Hordes coming from North! West! Air China! Tourist bus! Think Forbearden City Gift Shop is new Walbeart! Quiet in bruin ranks! Quick to display selves on shelves! And smile as if your very stitches depend on it!

34

MARK

Day 31 Friday March 22nd 2002

I had an amazing afternoon at The Forbidden City. Our guide I-Sho-Yu showed us a sampling of the 3000 years of Chinese art, from ancestor paintings to the dynastic masters of drawing and painting flowers, horses, birds, even modern still lifes. Absolutely superb overview. A super day, except it was pretty scary at the end. I thought I'd lost Gus in the check-in area of the gift shop. A clerk finally found my knapsack. Tossed, of course. Nothing missing but Gus. Took me a long time, but I found him in the stock room under this jumble of stuffed animals, some dressed in outfits with funny, five-clawed green dragons on them.

GUS

My true mission in China was revealed today. I am not here merely to enhance my skills in The Three Bearfections. I came here to teach the small, but Last Emperbear of China the superior ways of the West: our stuffiness, our overbearingly happy families, our super bear hugs and cub schools. I was glad when the guards made Mark leave his knapsack and me behind. Let Mark explore the palace workshops, museums, pavilions and gardens.

I was privileged to spend time in the small violet-purple room, where Imbearial Denizens like Dragon Ladybear and Pu-I-Win display themselves by day and live furrily by night. Later, I especially enjoyed chatting with one cute concubear wearing a violet robe. Anyway, she was going on and on about their new court musician, also from the West, named Bearthoven or Mozart Bear.

MADAMA BEARTTERFLY: He has composed the most exquisite chambear music for baby bears and bearnotas for nanny bears and has promised to write special music for my beartterfly dance at the Spring Festival.

GUS

I didn't have the gall-bladder to tell her this guy probably was not the real Bearthoven or whoever, but a cheap knock-off. I was about to ask her if I might visit again when an imposing figure, looking a lot like our Shirley Holmes, stepped out from behind the screen.

JUDGE DEE: I am the Honorable Chief Magistrate, Judge Dee, and you are?

GUS: Gus Greenbear, tutor to Pu-I-Win, small, but . . .

GUS

He grabbed me by the scruff of my neck and escorted me out.

GUS: Wait, you're just the guy I need to help me find the Fortune Cookie Recipe Scroll. Hey fella, no need for the rough stuff.

OUT AND ABOUT

MARK

Day 37 Thursday March 28th 2002
My Chinese is so improved. To practice, I buy little things at stands that sell fruit, vegetables, and flowers.

GUS: We should buy this potted plant for the hotel room to celebrate spring!

MARK: Gus, I'm not good with plants.

GUS: *(Sighs.)* Look at this healthy plant! It will bloom soon, there are buds all over, just as we are blooming in our talents. We can name this plant Mai Mai. She will be one of our Chinese family. Mai Long, Mai Zhang Yang, Mai Mai: two brothers, one sister. We can give her to our teacher, Ten-Ten when we leave. Listen to Mai Mai sing . . . to flower or not to flower . . .

MARK: Gus, the cold wind blowing in from the north is affecting your judgment. You are wallowing in sentimentality.

GUS: *(Reciting.)*
  I have been in cold winds before,
      But I never sang
         With the wind from Sibearia
         And smiled at flowers
            In Bearjing before.

MARK: Poets. *(Sighs.)*

MARK

I must admit it's nice to have lovely red flowers on our window sill. We also painted Mai Mai for flower-drawing practice. Gus is solely responsible for her care, since I tend to over water.

38

THE GREAT WALL OF CHINA

MARK

Day 46 Saturday April 6th 2002
We had to climb like Spiderman up The Wall! Yes, The Great Wall of China. Or the G. Dubyah as Gus calls it. No, not the usual tourist trek, but the broken-down, rough section, which starts near the ocean at the coastal city Quinghuandao, six hours by train from Beijing. Our kung-fu teacher invited us to join him. He teaches Tae Kwan Do there on weekends.

GUS

We were eager to climb where The Wall first enters the mountains.

MARK

What better place to see The Great Wall than at the beginning!
I've seen lots of monuments before, from America to Iraq, but
this one is . . . monumental! We took some exciting photos:
Gus hanging out of the train, Gus hanging by one paw from the
Wall, Gus . . .

GUS

. . . on a magnificent stallion!

MARK

. . . on this old nag that people could sit on and take pictures.
I asked the guy in my broken Chinese how much it costs, and
he says in very good English that it costs three dollars to
stand by the horse and five dollars to sit on him. Of course
Gus wanted to ride, so I paid five dollars, put Gus in the saddle
and stood by the horse. I didn't know Gus was so fond of horses.

GUS

Far down to the sandy beach, I see this little caravan, crawling nearer and nearer. Looks like two old palanquins with green dragons painted on the sides, carried by puffing bearers, some royalty behind the curtains? The little guys strutting behind must be the Wei Brothers. Bringing up the rear is Fu-I-Dog chasing his tail. Leading the procession on his motorcycle is Mai Shu wearing gold armor. Pu-I-Win, small, but last Emperbear was in the sidecar. Where are they going, I wonder? I'll just gallop on down there. Whoooooaaa!

DRAGON LADYBEAR: Hai! Halt! Stop! Stop! Dragon Ladybear orders stopping! Time to consult with great brawny bear in gold armor, Yellow Emperbear, which way to go as we come bearing gifts to the Blessed Bearddha from Bearindia. I am dizzy traveling in yin-yang circles through water, fire, earth, metal, and piney woods. I order stopping to get bearings.

GUS: Hai.

YELLOW EMPERBEAR: Oh, hi Gus.

GUS: Mai Shu? Is that you? What's with the gold armor? Wait a minute, I know you. I don't just watch TV, I read books. I know some Bearnese bear stories. You are the Yellow Emperbear, the First Emperbear. You lived 4,700 years ago, created the BPS and other cool stuff. What are you doing here with Dragon Ladybear and Pu-I-Win, the small, but very Last Emperbear? Are you, are we in some other lifetime when you, Mai Shu were the Yellow Emperbear? Help me out here.

YELLOW EMPERBEAR: *(Polishing his goggles.)* Hai! Yellow Emperbear is my bearginning in panda fur. Life is cycle, unbroken tai chi. Life is yin-yang, light-dark, large-small, all rainbear colors.

WEI BROTHERS: As Confuse-us say, "Just when you think it's over, China's bearly begun."

PU-I-WIN: Hai! And remember story of eight bears who follow Tao, the "Way," and learn to become live forever. I will follow Yellow Bear Road like Eight Immortals. I will be Last Emperbear forever!

DRAGON LADYBEAR: Hai! Dowager Empress Dragon Ladybear orders starting! Follow Yellow Bear Road.

MADAMA BEARTTERFLY: Hai! Help, help, O help! O, Walking Dragon, O, Green Pilgrim Bear, lend me your ears. Pause for sad song from Madama Beartterfly, being bearnapped from violet room in Forbearden City. Dragon Ladybear and Yellow Emperbear want to silence my heart songs. Driving them bonkers. They pay B.J. the Pirate King to keep me forever on tourist junk. This same guy steal fortune cookie recipe from palace long ago and sell it to Ambearican Walbeart. They hold Fortune Cookie Franchise in all Chinese restaurants in Abearica. Now I must sail with pirate king in pirate junk on Yellow River 2,000 miles, like Wandering Bear of myth and legend. Sing, sing all stuffed ones, great and small, O pitiful tale of Madama Beartterfly . . .

(All hum part of the "Humming Chorus."
The horse whinnies and Fu-I-Dog humph-aarfs.)

GUS: Have no fear. I'll save you, sweet Lady Vi . . . Beartterfly!

MARK: Sorry Little Buddy. Time's up.

GUS: Rats!

GUS

Time on my war steed was up. Whisked into Mark's backpack and with miles to go on the G. Dubyah before I can sleep and dream of a rescue plan, I call out to her.

GUS: Hai! Be brave, sweet concubear.

GUS

The last sounds I heard were a snatch of opera music, Mai Shu's motorcycle clawing itself out of the sand, and the Yellow Emperbear growling out directions.

YELLOW EMPERBEAR: Teddies, when in forest, bear left . . . unless it's right.

KUNG-FU CLASS

MARK

Day 48 Monday April 8th 2002
Is it my imagination, or is Gus becoming more aggressive and more mellow at the same time? Uh oh. A bi-polar bear? A mid-bear crisis? Homesick, I mean hugsick for his special bear? Lady Violet?

GUS

What's going on with Mark? Late at night, he watches full-contact fighting called Sanda on TV, says he "loves it" 'cause "they beat the stuffing out of each other." Then, today in kung-fu class, when I want to learn a new form with this big fork, he gets all nanny-prissy-over-protective.

MARK: Gus, no respectable bear would use such a weapon. The trident was used by Poseidon, the Greek god of the seas. He had fish scales for skin, oysters and barnacles in his beard and seaweed and corals for hair.

GUS: *(Under his breath.)* Poets.

MARK

He's sad again. Oops, oysters. Maybe they made Gus think of the little pearl necklace lovely Lady Violet wears. Her pale-pink paws that soothe his furrowed brow as she offers British breakfast beargrass tea.

GUS: Mark, let me remind you that polar bears can swim for hundreds of miles at a time and are worthy of both godships and tridents. Besides, in China the trident is called the tiger fork because it was used to combat tigers in the mountains, villains in the fields, oppressors of the poor in the cities, river pirates who sneak their boats onto sandy shores where pale-pawed maidens in violet kimonos crane their agile necks to see stars.

MARK: Poets! A tiger fork is huge, even for people, much less a teddy bear. I think you haven't found the best form or weapon-of-choice to fit your personality. We work out everyday. The teachers push hard and expect much. We give it to them, too. Right, Gus? After all, we are Walking Dragon and Soldier Who Walks in the Sun.

GUS: Roger that. Oorah!

AT THE MARKET

MARK

Day 49 Tuesday April 9th 2002

Today was a really good day. I sparred with my Tae Kwan Do teacher. He is so fast and so strong with his feet that all I could do was block and punch. He kicked me in the head two times, got me once really good in my tofu belly. Didn't hurt, tofu power. Oorah!

I punched him good once, and I threw him twice. But overall, he beat me good. It was fun. They also had the drunken boxing elective today, but . . .

GUS

We didn't stay for that class. Instead, we went to a huge shopping market.

MARK

Bottom floor, meat products, everything from live turtles to Peking-duck heads in buckets. I walked really fast past the vendors who had real bear parts to sell for use in love potions.

GUS: You know, Mark, people don't realize how nice it is that teddies don't have gender issues. A ribbon in the right place, a hardhat on a furry head, mix and match. We can play all positions on any team. Look at Kwan Yin Bear, Bearddhism's Merciful Compassionate One. She started out with only two arms like a grizzly, but as more and more cubs gathered around her for blessings of honey, statues of her started looking like motherbears everywhere, who have 100 arms and 1000 eyes.

GUS

Mark was so busy looking at stuff that he didn't even hear me.

MARK

Third floor had every kind of electronic equipment one could imagine. Fourth floor had loads of stuffed pandas.

GUS

Mark bought us matching T-shirts: black with a red phoenix and a dragon dancing in a circle. I put mine on right away. Mark put his in the bag with . . .

MARK

Some art books, and socks. I bought ten pairs of fun socks, 100% cotton, for under ten dollars. Oorah!

GUS

While Mark was loading up on socks, I found my weapon-of-choice. Paid for it and slipped it into Mark's bag. It is eleven inches high, only an inch taller than me. Instead of a tiger fork, it has a three-inch single-edged blade. And this is the best part, a walking dragon is etched on the blade.

Our teacher says the Chinese call this weapon a Kwan Do because it was created by this famous general named, that's right, General Kwan. Fit only for high-level beartial artists like me, no matter what Mark thinks.

MARK

Books and socks! More socks and books! What a great day. Thank goodness I am an art student who likes to look at pictures rather than read someone else's thoughts on the pictures because there aren't many Chinese art books in English. I did get a couple myth books in English that I started reading to Gus at night.

MARK: Little Buddy, there is this really great story about a legendary Yellow Emperor back at the very beginning of Chinese history, who invented all this stuff, like writing, the compass, the pottery wheel. "He became a magician at 100 years old and finally achieved immortality by riding on a dragon to heaven."

MARK

Gus fell asleep before I got to the part he would have liked the best.

MARK: "The Yellow Emperor is most famous for having an army of bears, tigers, and other ferocious animals that conquered armies of demons." *(Softly.)* Oorah! Sleep well, Gus, Little Buddy, Mai Long. I'll bearmark this page for you.

AT THE HOTEL

& OUT AND ABOUT

MARK
Day 50 April 10th 2002
White Flags!

GUS

Mark and I have called a truce on our fierce competition to reach The Three Bearfections of Chinese art. I have agreed not to burst out in bear-belly laughs at Mark's inept use of poetic language.

MARK

I will quit bearbaiting Gus about his poor paw-stroke paintings, and unbearable calligraphy. We decided to enjoy the simple things, our comfortable room and the politeness of the staff. I make the bed every morning, the soldier's way I was trained in the Army, and every morning the maid looks at me, smiles and says how poorly I do her job. That's only speculation on my part, as I don't understand most of her Chinese, but she always remakes the bed. The Chinese take their jobs very seriously. No tipping please.

GUS

Even at this restaurant Mark really likes, Mr. Pizza, the employees rush to greet us. Then they form a line to our table so we don't get lost.

MARK

I point to the picture in the menu, small veggie pizza and a coke. The waiter brings it right out, four dollars, "No tipping please."

GUS

I leave behind all my practice drawings on napkins as a bonus. Sometimes I even add a bit of mustard and catsup as washes for my art since the favorite Chinese colors are yellow and red.

48

MARK

Four dollars. You can't beat the price, especially since Gus tends to make a mess at most any restaurant.

KUNG-FU STUDIO

GUS
We are very supportive of each other in our martial-arts study. Mark now realizes how serious I am about learning to use my weapon-of-choice, the Kwan Do.

MARK
We took an elective class today and learned a new form called tumbling boxing. It is soooooo hard. One part is handsprings, only from our heads. It starts with five no-handed kip ups . . .

GUS: Then four headsprings in a row.

MARK: One flip over and land on your back from a standing position . . .

GUS : Three flying kicks . . .

MARK: Two turtle doves . . .

GUS : Three red hens . . .

MARK: And some other cool stuff.

GUS & MARK: Oorah! Oorah!

MARK

Back at the hotel we stretched out on my Lucky-Ducky comforter and read another great myth story. This one was about a half-dragon, half-human hero named Yu, who transformed himself into a bear so he could carry these huge, heavy stones for an irrigation system that would drain off flood waters into the sea. Gus loved it. I read another good tale about the legendary Jade Emperor who knew 72 ways of transforming himself. He finally became an immortal. There was another story about a celestial dog who warned everybody about evil spirits. He looked like the dog I bought at Taco Bell and who now lives in Gus' hug. Go figure.

(Gus' snores are mixed with soft "humphs.")

FIELD TRIP!

MARK

Day 52 Friday April 12th 2002
Our last weekend field trip took us south of Beijing into the Chinese countryside. It was all around fantastic. We ate too much, laughed a lot, got a bunch of sun and much more.

On the overnight train to Zhengzhou there were six men, five women in our university group, and then seventy-eleven young school kids got onboard, each one with a stuffed animal in a backpack . . .

GUS

. . . And Mai Shu's Shanghai Bearpaws returning home after winning the national bearball finals in Sibearia. So much noise! But it wasn't just the pandas partying on too much bamboo juice. I saw a lot of familiar muzzles under their disguises of pilgrim robes, Dragon Ladybear and her Hug. Among the strangers in Harley leathers and Hawaiian leis, I spotted two fine-looking fellows who stood out from the rest. One bear looked like Greeley, my green protégé in our Hug back home. The other bear reminded me of Nelson, a teddy stuffed in South Africa. I sensed they would play an important part in the days ahead.

MARK

The train arrived in Zhengzhou at 5 a.m. *(Yawns.)* We cleaned up and ate a big breakfast at our three-star hotel.

GUS: *(Mutters.)* But alas, no green eggs and ham. Rice, morning rice, noon rice, evening rice.

MARK

We traveled by bus to an ancient city named Kaifeng, east of Zhengzhou, that had an old Forbidden City. There was one temple there that had hundreds of bonsai trees in it, also a Buddhist temple with a statue of the goddess of mercy, Kwan Yin, carved from a 1000 year old ginkgo tree. Kwan Yin had 1000 arms and hands, with eyes in the palms. She smiled sort of like my grandmother.

BEAR-CUB SCHOOL

GUS

I was most impressed by my visit to an adjoining bear-cub school. We were allowed to sit in on an early bear-care class. Comrade Teacher was a brisk, clever instructor, cousin of our very own Shirley Holmes, who here in China passed her literary examinations to become Chief Magistrate Judge Dee. She kept insisting that the cubs, who look a lot like our Wee Bears, follow clues.

COMRADE TEACHER: Hai! Look! Look deep, this way, that way. Colors have meaning. Red, blue, yellow, not just red, blue, yellow. Analyze, find deeper meaning. I tell no bear story until you learn colors. This crayon is red. Tell me what red mean in all bear lifetimes.

CUBS: *(Raising their paws and shouting out answers.)* Hai! Red mean sun. Red mean dragon. Fire of phoenix. Red mean New Year happiest lucky-ducky day.

COMRADE TEACHER: And in modern much improved Republic of China? What mean red?

CUB: Hai! Little-red Bear-book.

COMRADE TEACHER: This is blue. What mean blue?

CUBS: Blue mean Heaven. Ocean. Azure Dragon of East. True blue wise one, Blessed Bearddha from Bearindia. Bearjing smog cause blue moon in night sky. Clear blue day for Olympics!

COMRADE TEACHER: This is yellow crayon. What mean yellow?

CUBS: Yellow mean Earth. Home sweet den. Yellow River. Long, long ago mean Yellow Emperbear. Yellow mean honey-money from Walbeart in Abearica.

GUS

At that point, this little bear, green as a lucky cricket, points its paw at where I was sitting quietly at the back and says . . .

CUB: Hai. He's green! He's green like me! Comrade Teacher tell us again, what green mean?

COMRADE TEACHER: Ah so, ah so, story time. All bear tales in book *Romance of the Three Kingdoms*. Middle Chinese history. We lucky-duckies! We have three lucky green bears here today. We can do Chinese play about brothers of the green wood. Many paw claps now for first greenbear, name of Robinbear before he become Bearnese god of war, Kwan Yu. Get many temples now. Many paw claps for Kwan Yu!

CUBS: Robinbear! Superbear! General Kwan Yu! Kwan Di! Kwan Do! We call you million names!

COMRADE TEACHER: Next, many paw claps for Green Squirebear and Greenson of Kwan Yu, god of war.

GREENSON BEAR: I, Greenson Bear bow to you, O Revered Fatherbear. Knock head three times to show how bravely I fight many battles by your side.

GREENSQUIRE BEAR: I, your most brave Green Squirebear bow to you, O Green Master. Knock head three times to show how I carry your heavy weapon-of-choice, Kwan Do, many miles, *(Mutters.)* like Mark carry Gus in backpack.

GUS

So, suddenly, I am Kwan Yu, god of war, revered by these two strapping green teddies looking even bigger than they did on the train. And here we are, in front of these tiny little cubs who already know the Peach Orchard bear tale of the "Brothers of the Green Woods." How I, Robinbear, who started out in a family of bean-curd peasants, got into this grunting argument with a traveling bean-curd salesbear when a straw-sandaled green teddy stepped in between us and eventually we all became beary good friends called the Brothers of the Green Woods and swore oaths to help each other out of trouble as long as we had any fur left. As centuries went on, this story got all pawed about, and I became General Kwan, a father with a green son and a green squire fighting these clan battles! You know how war stories always get blown up. I guess it's the Chinese Dream, start out as a green bean-curd farmer, and end up with temples dedicated to you as a great Chinese Bear Idol!

COMRADE TEACHER: Tell story again, O Great Green Ones, bear story how Kwan Yu saved young ladybear from bearnappers . . .

GREENSQUIRE BEAR: Actually, as the powerful squire carting the heavy Kwan Do around, and since I was the green bear who had mastered the most wushu moves, it was I who ended up slaying most of the bearnappers and dragons and . . .

GREENSON BEAR: Wait a minute! Young green son is the real hero. I was tops in den school, and got loads of medals in the Cub Scouts on how to use magical green bear powers to overcome the demons that were fighting alongside the Yellow River bearnappers . . .

CUBS: *(Encouraging a fight.)* Bearbaiting! Bearbaiting! Green bears, fight, fight, fight with mighty paws and claws!

GUS

Well, when I tried to stop this, stepped in between these pushy-pullybully-green-bruins shoving and gouging, my hot, Abearican, bearserker blood began to boil, my muzzle fur started turning bright red . . .

COMRADE TEACHER: Look! Look! See red! See red! And that, cubs, how Kwan Yu able to slip past all guarded bearriers! When muzzle turn to red, guard bears no recognize Kwan Yu. That is how he rescue lady-bear from bearnappers.

(wild cheers!)

THE YELLOW RIVER

MARK

After we prayed at the temples, we went to eat a big lunch at a three-star hotel, where I noticed Gus had some red stuff on his face. At first, I thought it was catsup, but when I tried to get him cleaned up, I realized that it was oil-based colored pencil. Then we headed off to an old pumping station turned tourist site, on the middle arm of, surprise, the Yellow River! We hiked up a nearby mountain and looked way down to the river. We could see why our guide called this China's "cradle of civilization," and . . .

GUS

Militarily strategic! It didn't take a General Kwan Yu to recognize a good harbor. There were tents and boats. Lots of boats! Boats with colored flags bearing crossed bear claws on a yellow dragon background and pirate bears swarming all over the decks of a fancy Chinese junk.

(Hearing strains of the "Humming Chorus.")

Is that Madama Beartterfly being bearhandled by pirates?

MARK

Maybe there's a river festival going on down by the water. We could hear some music even as far away as we were. There were banners, and tents and boats and lots of swarming about. We watched for quite awhile. Then, some of us practiced our martial-art forms right there on the mountain. I've finally realized that all my teachers were right about trying to be accomplished in too many new forms too fast. I've studied four forms, but today I did just the mantis and Gus the nanchuan.

GUS
("Humming Chorus" is building in volume.)

But I knew this was not a practice session for me anymore. Madama Beartterfly was in really big bear trouble. So I threw on my armor, grabbed up my Kwan Do, mounted my warhorse and galloped on down to the river.

56

YELLOW EMPERBEAR: Hai! General Kwan Yu! Thank Mao Bear-tung you have arrived.

PU-I-WIN: Hai! And thank Confuse-us and Pooh-Tao.

YELLOW EMPERBEAR: Ah, reinforcements have arrived. General Kwan Yin is running fast, followed by her Army and the Wei Brothers.

WEI BROTHERS: Hai! Yellow Emperbear and General Kwan Yu thank Blessed Bearddha from Bearindia we found you.

GENERAL KWAN YIN: *(Panting.)* Hai! Hai, hai, hai. And may Kwan Yin have mercy on bad pirates because we everyday commubears won't! Ladybears, throw off your ribbons, your necklaces of pearls and jade. Break those chains . . . of daisies, violets, roses. Remember, you are not human! No arms deals. No hanky-panky. No fooly-drooly meal deals. No honey-money. All teddies are equal. We are bears, hear us roar! See my strong arm? Really 1000 arms, the arms of Kwan Yin! Together, we can do it!

YELLOW EMPERBEAR: We are ready to follow you General Rosie-the-Riveter Kwan Yin and you General Kwan Yu and his son and squire carrying his weapon-of-choice. Come on down to the river, Mai Long! Yes, you, Gus Greenbear! Be great General Kwan Yu, help Yellow Emperbear and Dragon Ladybear rescue Madama Beartterfly from B.J. the Pirate King and his bearnappers.

GENERAL KWAN YIN: Give no quarter to Yellow River Pirates, wearing lovely yellow scarves.

GUS: Yellow? I thought yellow was reserved for the Imbearial color? And I thought Dragon Ladybear and Yellow Emperbear paid this B.J. to bearnap Beartterfly?

DRAGON LADYBEAR: Hai! Ha, mysterious East. Which side is everybody on? Who is a good bear, bad bear? Why? Where? When? You see us. Yellow Emperbear, Pu-I-Win, small, but last Emperbear and I—Dowager Empress Dragon Ladybear so powerful bear brains behind throne for 40 years. See how Confuse-us, Pooh-Tao, Blessed Bearddha from Bearindia, Comrade Mai Shu in motorcycle eyes holding Little-red Bear-book, all here same time, same place. Look! Pirate vessel dead ahead. Now is always best time.

GENERAL KWAN YIN: Board her. General Kwan Yu, you take my cutlass. Your weapon-of-choice way too long for close-quarter fighting with B. J. the Pirate King. And remember I get the first dance with Madama Beartterfly at wrap party.

GUS: But, but she's my Lady Violet.

ALL BEARS: Crack! Clash! Slash! Boom!

(Shouts of victory.)

GENERAL KWAN YU: On your knees P. J.

B.J. THE PIRATE KING: B. J. Not P.J. Long-ago name "Peking Pirate" before "Bearjing, the Pirate King." I have relatives in Abearica called the Pittsbear Pirates.

GENERAL KWAN YU: Stop. Before I hang you from the yardarm tell me where . . .

58

GENERAL KWAN YIN: My job, Boss. Yardarms, all arms my job. I can do it.

GENERAL KWAN YU: Where is the fortune cookie recipe scroll?

GENERAL KWAN YIN: I make him talk, boss, with rivet gun.

B.J. THE PIRATE KING: No rivets, I'll talk. Gus Greenbear, you will find answer in own bearheart. Tonight in three-star hotel dreams? Tomorrow in Magic Kingdom Shaolin Temple? In stars in violet sky? I give you one beary good clue. On one claw hangs the answer to the mystery. Tomorrow and tomorrow and tomorrow . . . ?

MARK

After a short, but surprising trip to a Jewish quarter where Mandarin-speaking, Chinese Jews trace their synagogue back to 1163, we were tired. So we went to eat our big dinner at another three-star hotel. Then we went to our own three-star hotel room where I read some chapters from *The Romance of the Three Kingdoms,* a story called the "Dream of the Violet Chamber." Gus was out after two pages, but I read a long time until the people, the dynasties, the philosophies all blurred together. I finally fell asleep and didn't wake up until this cheesy kung-fu movie came on the TV. Pows! Bams! Oorah! Gus and I got cleaned up and went down to breakfast.

GUS

Cakes with icing and everything. What, no rice?

MARK

Way too much breakfast again. Then on to The Shaolin Kung-Fu School for a demonstration by the monks.

THE SHAOLIN TEMPLE

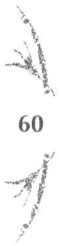

GUS
At the Shaolin Temple we saw a 1400 year old ginkgo tree, with holes in the trunk created by bear monks making their claws sharper by scratching.

MARK: "The ginkgo is a living fossil?" This guy's family goes back two hundred million years. Some family tree, eh Little Buddy?

MARK

Then we saw a pagoda forest supposed to be the largest one in China. Impressive! The buildings all appeared to be old and presumably the originals. But we found out that they were in fact, new reproductions of the old buildings. The old ones were destroyed many times. With the crush of people everywhere, I never felt closer to but farther away from Disney World. And I'm certain that Buddha hasn't been here for hundreds of years. Well, enough of the profane.

GUS

Even though many people and teddies walked through the forest snapping pictures and leaving pawprints, the place still felt sacred to me. A place where Pu-I-Win, the Wei Brothers and all stuffed animals, made in China, might come for prayers.

MARK

Outside the temple I got this great bargain, a hanging scroll. The vendor hawking it looked like a pirate. Forty bucks, but it was worth it. Better quality than any I've seen in Beijing. I like it a lot. Three figures, one in a green robe sat on a throne. A fierce-faced guy holding a Kwan Do stood behind him and this younger looking guy stood beside him. I may gift it to my kung-fu teacher, Sifu, back in Tampa. Oh, I took some exciting photos: Gus in the hands of the Father of Chinese Medicine healing the Yellow Emperor, Gus in a dragon's mouth, Gus in trouble again . . .

GUS

After the Shaolin Temple visit, we had a two-hour drive back to Zhengzhou. We only had an hour before the train left, so the group had dinner at a restaurant in a two-star hotel. Mark ate too much again. And alas, no fortune cookie.

AT THE HOTEL

MARK

Day 49 Monday April 15th 2002
Back into Beijing at 5:10 a.m. Overall, the weekend was wonderful, especially my favorite part—the Yellow River tour. I think I'll sleep, but not too long, I have a Chinese lesson at 1:30 and a wushu class tonight. I'm exhausted, but I must make it through the day, plenty of time to sleep tonight.

GUS

Mark's denned in today, on his lucky-Ducky comforter, like he thinks it's still winter hibearnation or something. It's April! No spring sleeping, no bearnaps for me!
My head is buzzing like bees on a honeycomb. I'm busy, scratching out ideas for poems and plays and stuff.
Lots of Chinese bear stories to draw from, like the one I heard on the train about the Jade Emperbear. I'll play that part, though I know two green guys in my hug who

would fight me for it. And what about that Dragon Ladybear who was the only ribboned teddie to rule in her own name sometime in the something dynasty? Rosie Beara could play that part. Our Wee Bears love to dress up. Dino, Chilly and Scuba Steve can be her retainers. Lady Violet can take over the part of that cute little concubear stolen by bearnappers. And I'm thinking a series of mysteries with Shirley Holmes as the legendary Chief Magistrate, Judge Dee, which reminds me I am no closer to finding the ancient scroll with the fortune cookie recipe.

MARK

I've got a great idea for an art piece. Gus on a warhorse. The title, I think, will be "Gus Playing General Kwan." I've been planning, drawing all morning. I mostly stole the composition from that old scroll I bought. And I'm thinking big, four by four on wood. First, I'll do a contour drawing on the wood, then carve the lines in it, and fill them with oil-based color pencil. I'll sand the wood down, then use acrylic, or waterproof ink-washes to color the drawing, red, yellow and green. My duck talisman tucked in somewhere. I want to achieve an old-faded-scroll look. I may sand some color off . . . I won't know until I get there. This is the early stage, and there's plenty of room for it to go south. As a wise Chinese-Abearican poet once told me, "Just because your language has pauses and clauses, don't think you've Papa Bear!"

GUS

Claws! That was B.J.'s clue. The scroll is hanging on a claw in the wall. Boy, am I glad Mark didn't pack up the scroll. He's been studying it for days now and drawing like mad in his scratchbook. Now that he's at his Chinese lesson it's my turn. Boy oh boy these guys sure look familiar. Nothing on the front. Maybe, on the back. No. The backing has started to peel, maybe I can just help it along and see. Well wow, look at this tiny scroll with writing on it stuck half-way up. This is it all right. I just know it. I'm one lucky ducky. I gotta find Mai Shu and get this translated. Then I'll make a photocopy of the original, paste it in my scratchbook, grab a cab and take the original to Dragon Ladybear at the Palace. Oops, I better glue down the backing and sand the edges, so Mark won't notice that I was messing with his scroll.

Maybe Dragon Ladybear will order the palace cooks to make up a batch of fortune cookies for our wrap party tomorrow night.

MARK
Day 62 Monday April 22nd 2002
Our last day in China.

MARK: Gus, we leave here tomorrow—Tuesday April 23rd—and arrive home the same day three hours later. Can you believe it? It's because the earth is spinning so fast.

GUS: Yeah, I know.

GUS
Mark was surprised that I wasn't as surprised by that fact as he was. The most exciting thing is that we get to celebrate Shakesbear's birthday twice, once with raspberry champagne on the plane and then with blueberry muffins home at The Parrot House with our hug. Even better would be to ask Motherbear to cook up some fortune cookies from the 5000 year old recipe. I will do up the fortunes in calligraphy, which has improved under Ten-Ten's tutelage. Wait! How do I get the fortune inside the cookie? The Imperial cooks threw me out of the kitchen before I got to see that part. Motherbear is smart; she'll help me figure it out.

AIRPLANE FLIGHT
BEIJING TO TAMPA

MARK

Long flight. Seems longer coming home to Tampa than going to Beijing, but we needed time to begin processing all that we saw and did. And I needed time to figure out why the panda kept pushing this fishy story about the Republic not allowing computer geek teddies access to the interbearnet and stuff.

66

GUS

I needed time to convince the nervous runaway that everybody in Abearica just loves pandas. They pay big bucks to get even a tiny look. I told that panda over and over how he would be welcomed into our hug in Bearami.

MAI SHU: No hugging. Abearicans are such huggers.

GUS: I'll warn Lady Violet and the two Rosies about no bear hugs, but don't count on that lasting more than a week. And Mai Shu, stop fooling with Mark's head. Give up already with that geek bear story. He doesn't buy it.

MARK

I know what's really going on here, and I feel for the guy. Defecting from China is a protest against a powerful government that has denied his right to protest. He's probably been arrested a couple of times at Tiananmen Square, right in front of the Forbidden City. Before we go through Customs I feel morally obligated to check out his butt.

MAI SHU: Hey fella. Hands off!

GUS

Mai Shu was embearassed. But he calmed down a bit when I reminded him of Ten-Ten's story of his travel restrictions due to butt bearings.

MAI SHU: Gus, please keep my secret about the jade necklace at least until I trust Mark more. You see, when we rescued Madama Beartterfly from her floating beardoir, she gave me this jade necklace as a reminder of my promise to return someday to the Yellow River.

GUS

I was beary jealous. See, in my mind that cute little concubear is my Lady Violet. This is the thanks I get for stealing back her pearl necklace, which B.J. the Pirate King snatched from her neck when he put her in the brig. I had to fight that dastardly pirate bear in the rigging to wrench those pearls away from him. After I calmed down a bit, I thought of a diversion . . .

GUS: Mai Shu, you may not want to go back to China. Wait till you meet Lady Fern from Hotlanta. Her honey-tongue will charm those jade beads right off your neck. You'll love The Parrot House, but you may not like the trip home. Mark is going to ship us from Tampa home to Bearami Box Class.

MAI SHU: I've been in close-quarter dens before and some really tight situations. I'm okay with that. Or we could get a motorcycle and be in Bearami by nightfall.

GUS: A motorcycle trip. Wow! Let's do it. *(To Mark)* Mark, stop fidgeting. You worry too much. The denhug security check at the Tampa Bearport will be a piece of cake. Do some art or write about the mysteries of the green jade or something.

MARK: I'm thinking about writing a poem to close my China Journal. You may not appreciate it. It's not one of your precious forms like hokku, haiku, tanka or whatever. But I haven't given up on "The Three Perfections" . . .

MARK

Okay, here's the story. See, when I was 18, I was a soldier, Desert Storm in Iraq. I flew there over the North Pole, over Russia. But I didn't see Alaska and Russia covered in snow. On this trip I did. This is my memory from our journey to China. This is my poem:

Gus said he saw a polar bear.
> I think a glare walked in his eyes instead.

> > Signed, Mai Zhang Yang, humble poet.

ALL: (Shouting.) Poets! Oorah!

THE END

Mark's China Trip Scrapbook

Dragon Wall

Gus' jade
Walking
Dragon
totem

Gus ready to be shipped Box Class-Miami to Tampa

Gus in Flight to Beijing, China

With Gus in front of the Xi Jiao Hotel, Beijing, China

Gus checking out the view from our hotel window

The Fairy Fountain

Yuanming Yuan
Landscape
Gardens
Beijing

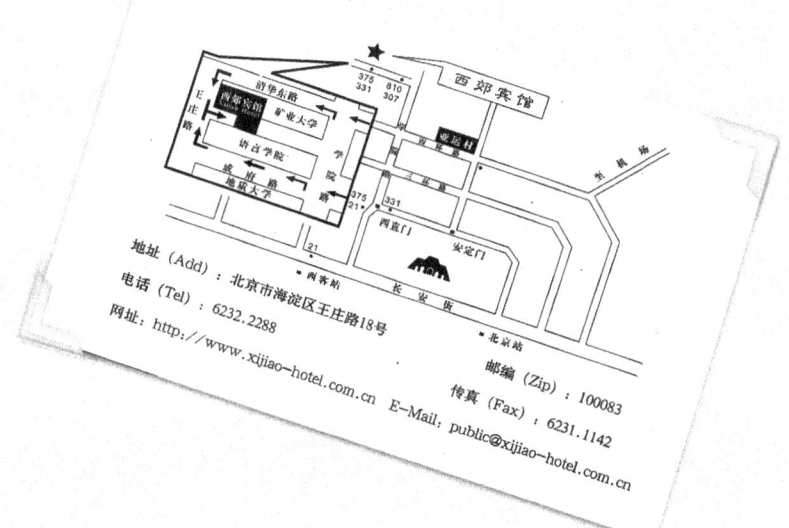

地址（Add）：北京市海淀区王庄路18号

电话（Tel）：6232.2288

网址：http://www.xijiao-hotel.com.cn

邮编（Zip）：100083

传真（Fax）：6231.1142 E-Mail: public@xijiao-hotel.com.cn

Gus working out
in the park

Gus spending quality time on The Lucky-Ducky comforter

古斯绿熊

Gus practicing to improve his beastly paw strokes and just bearable calligraphy

北京留学世界广场

Beijing Foreign Student Activities Center

地址：北京市海淀区志新西路 3-1 号
No. 3-1 ZhixinxiRd; Haidian District Beijing
Tel: (8610) 62325577   62341155 - 0/1104
Fax: (8610) 62320450   Zip code: 100083
Contacted Person: Miss Yu

Field Trip!!!

Gus on
the train
going to
The Great Wall

83

河南省邮电印刷厂 — 2000 年8 月18 日印制 印量:5 万枚
00001-50000

角山风景区

存 根 联

票价: 壹拾柒元   2000 秦地税

№ 000213

角 山 风 景 区

JIAOSHAN MOUNTAIN

地方税务局监制

2000 秦地税

№ 000213

副 券

票价 壹拾柒元

Gus sitting on the broken down rough section of
The Great Wall, or the G. Dubyah as Gus calls it

角山风景区

存 根 联

票价：17元

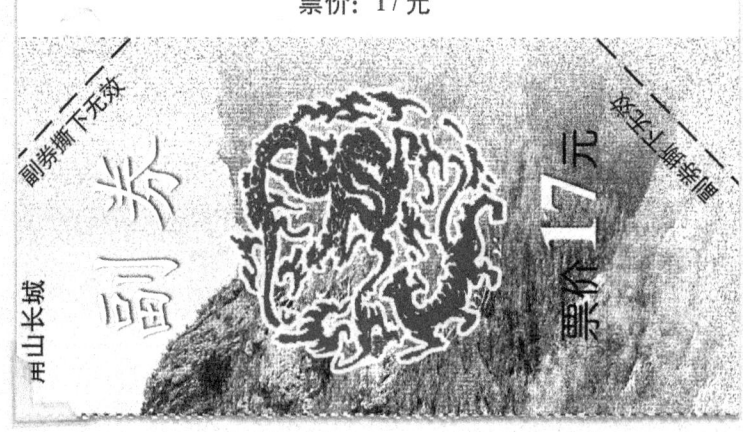

Carnival Game at Quinghuandao Plaza near The Great Wall.

Game to throw a bean bag at a stuffed animal or object.
"I will not throw anything at a fellow stuffie,"
said Gus, as he aimed at the objects on the right.

Gus with our Kung-Fu teacher

Our Kung-Fu teacher showing off his moves and weapons

Gus with his weapon-of-choice, The Kwan Do

At the monument of the
Yellow Emperor riding into the Sea

At the Yellow River Monument

Kwan Yin

had 1000 arms
and a smile sort of like my grandmother

The 1400 year old Ginkgo tree at the Shaolin Temple

Practicing the Mantis Pose on the mountain

A kung-fu pose called
Golden Rooster Stands on One Leg

Gus in the hands of
The Father of
Chinese Medicine,
healing the
Yellow Emperor

Gus singing
with the singer
who is singing
to the
Yellow Emperor

Gus in the Mouth of the Dragon

How did he
get up there?

Gus in trouble again with a new friend, Oski.

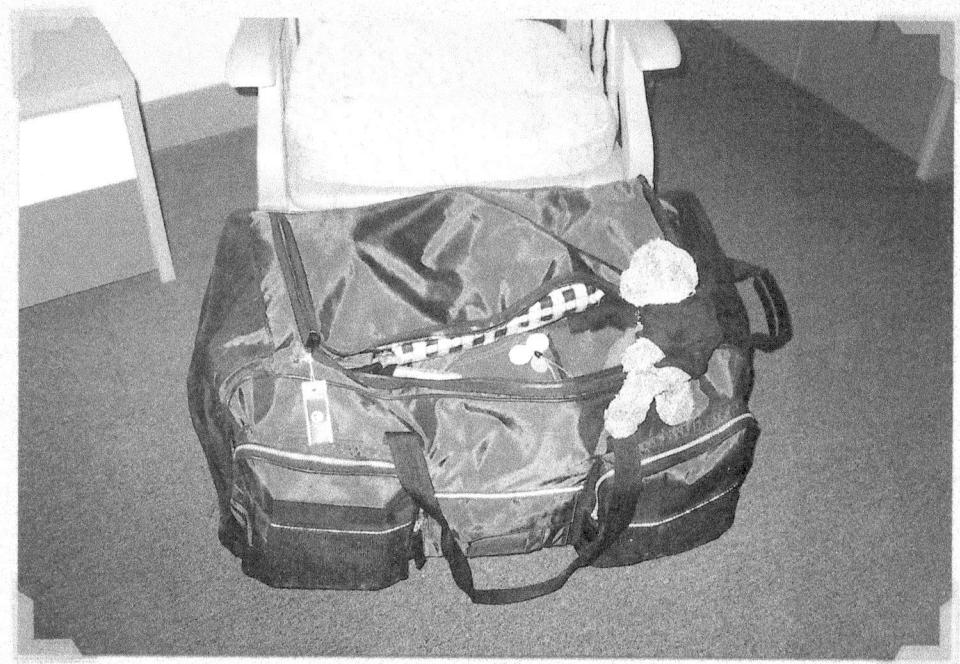

Gus packing his stuff to come home

Parrot House Hug's Welcome Home Party

Caper Pronunciation Guide

Page	Word	Sounds like
9	Mai Shu	my shoe
12	Xi Jiao	she jowl - without the l
14	Yuanming Yuan	yawnming yawn
16	hai	hi
22	Yuan	You-on or Ewan (like McGregor)
26	bagua	bahgwa
	Mai Long	my long
	Mai Zhang Yang	my jang yang
29	Hokku Haiku	hokoo hikoo
32	Kowtow	cowtow
	Tao	tow (cow with a t)
37	Mai Mai	my my
38	Quinghuandao	ching (like ping) whwa dow (cow with a d)
	Tae Kwan Do	tie kwan do (re, me, fa…)
44	Kwan Yin	kwan yin (tin with a y)
46	Kwan Do	kwan do (re, me, fa…)
50	Zhengzhou	jang jow (cow with a j)
52	Kaifeng	kaifung (Hi with a k and fungus without the us)
56	Mao	(cow with an m)
59	Shaolin	shaowlin

99

Biographies & Production Notes

The Authors

Sandra Riley—historian, novelist and playwright—and Peggy C. Hall—
an award-winning poet—live in Miami with a teddy bear named Gus
Greenbear. Gus appears in Peggy's books *Gus 'n Us* and *In Case of Bears*.
Gus also acted (he played himself) in the Crystal Parrot Players (2007-
2008) stage productions of Peggy's performance poetry, published
in 2010 as *Techno Poetry*. Gus told the story of his early years in
Sandra's book *The Greenbear Chronicles*. Recently Gus, grizzled wanna-be
pirate that he is, "impressed" Sandy, Peggy, Mark and Frank to finish
The Beijing Fortune Cookie Caper. He keeps everyone very busy. It is a wonder
that we get any of our other creative work done.

The Illustrators

My name is Aaren Johnson and I take the Computer Graphics course at Shorecrest Preparatory School as a member of the class of 2013. I have an amazing girlfriend named Molly, twin brothers, Cameron and Julian, and a baby brother, Mateo. For the illustrations of this book I used Adobe Photoshop CS3. By manipulating layers, tools, and filters I would mold different images to create cohesive pieces of art. I love creating art with Photoshop, and I also love how you can always learn something new with it whether you're a professional or an amateur. I plan to keep working with this for some time to come, and hopefully do some more books on the way!

My name is Alex Drexler. I am a member of the 2012 class at Shorecrest Preparatory School. The illustrations in the book were all created using Photoshop CS3 and CS5. We began by assembling a list of the ideas that would become the illustrations. We then photographed Gus and his friends in front of a green screen. Once we had all of the photos we needed, we brought them into Photoshop and began to integrate the bears into the scenes of the story. Using layers, masks, filters, gradients, and other tools we were able to bring to life the adventure of Gus and Mark's trip to China. The illustrations were such a success that I plan to make them the concentration of the Advanced Placement Art portfolio that I will be working on throughout my junior year.

The Instructor-Mark Runge

When I was first approached about the idea of having students illustrate a book, I knew immediately the names of the two kids that I would invite to participate. Much to my pleasure they agreed. We made a contract that the two students, Alex and Aaren, would use their class time to complete the project; the grade that they would receive for the class would be determined by their ability to communicate clearly with the authors, stay within the parameters of the authors' wishes, create an imaginative and cohesive body of illustrations, and do so within a specific amount of time. I cannot state how proud and pleased I am that Alex and Aaren far exceeded my expectations, and I would like to thank them for professionalism and the work that they produced. I would also like to thank Stephen Manella, the Principal of the Upper Division at Shorecrest Preparatory School in Saint Petersburg, FL, for allowing us to take on this project. And a heartfelt thanks must go to Sandy and Peggy, without whom our students would not have been able to shine through their work.

Designer's Notes

Cover

The title logo is a manipulated hand drawn brush face taken from a stencil set called Candy. It has the feel of Chinese brush work when manipulated in Adobe Photoshop and Illustrator. I researched iGoogles' translation service and used their Traditional Chinese characters for Gus Greenbear's name on the cover. The first two characters spell Gus and the other two spell Green and Bear respectively. But, for all I know it really says something unkind.

Typefaces

The book is both a narrative and a piece of art meant to be performed as well as read. I am a firm believer in the personality of typefaces to convey character traits and the tone of the book.

When Gus and Mark are writing rather than speaking, each has his own handwriting font. Gus' handwriting is a font called Chalkduster; it is clear and bold to portray his adventurous spirit. Mark's handwriting is Veneto and has the joyful flair of an artist. For the one e-mail they write, I used the standard Courier face which most Windows applications use to display e-mail messages in both print and mobile phone apps. We selected Stone Serif for all other body text because it is clear to read and "quiet" to look at.

Layout

The layout, designed for performance, allows Mark and Gus to fully express reactions to their journey of discovery. The character's name is centered when he delivers an interior monologue, narration or writes a journal entry. If the name is to the left, then the character is speaking to another character.

The opening scene is laid out in a way that conveys the dreamy inner mind of the characters as they fly from China back to the U.S.

Photography

I created a mock scrapbook album to hold Mark's photographs and accumulated ephemera. I simulated the photo corner mounts using Photoshop tools to create textures and manipulate their transparency. They always shift on me so why shouldn't Mark have the same problem? The scrapbook cover is a stock image from Graphic Authority. The inside cover is made from editing the cover image and adding a flysheet made from their antique papers collection. I turned a drawing made by Mark of his Lucky Duck "signature" into an emboss for the cover and a reverse emboss for the inside cover using Photoshop filters. The scrapbook pages are made using only the Photoshop noise filter. The pages are meant to simulate textured paper that a dual-purpose artist might use for both scrapbooking and drawing.

Book Design

I tweaked a traditional layout to create a book that irreverent, artist types might put together and bind themselves. And since some artists are ecology-minded, "Green" like Gus, I put the page numbers on the side to lengthen the text box allowing more content per page, thus saving paper.

PARROT HOUSE

BOOKS THAT ARE MEANT TO EDUCATE AND INSPIRE AS WELL AS ENTERTAIN